SITTING DUCKS

D0320816

For Liz and Jean-Paul with much love.
And to my parents, Joe and Lee,
who planted seeds in all the
empty spaces in my head.

Special thanks to Bob Commander for coming to the rescue.

First published 1998 in the United States by The Putnam & Grosset Group,
a division of Penguin Putnam Books for Young Readers, New York. Licensed by
Universal Studios Publishing Rights, a division of Universal Studios Licensing, Inc.
on behalf of Sitting Ducks Productions.

This edition with poster published 2002 by Walker Books Ltd
87 Vauxhall Walk, London SE11 5HJ

10 9 8 7 6 5 4 3 2

© 1998 Michael Bedard

This book has been typeset in Madama

Printed in Hong Kong

All rights reserved. No part of this book may be reproduced, transmitted
or stored in an information retrieval system in any form or by any means, graphic,
electronic or mechanical, including photocopying, taping and recording,
without prior written permission from the publisher.

British Library Cataloguing in Publication Data:
a catalogue record for this book is available
from the British Library

ISBN 0-7445-9422-7

SITTING DUCKS

Michael Bedard

WALKER BOOKS
AND SUBSIDIARIES
LONDON • BOSTON • SYDNEY

Day after day, a steady supply of ducks rolled off the assembly line at the Colossal Duck Factory. Alligators pushed buttons and pulled levers that kept the machines humming, while conveyor belts moved the ducks through the factory. Finally, the ducks were loaded on to trucks for their journey to the city. Rarely did anything go wrong.

But one day, an egg came through the incubation chamber unhatched. It rolled off the assembly line and fell down, down, down into the shadowy darkness below.

The egg landed with a loud crack on the factory floor. Dazed by this rude introduction to the world, a little duck emerged and surveyed his strange surroundings.

He wandered through
the forest of machinery,
awed by its size and dazzled
by its beauty.

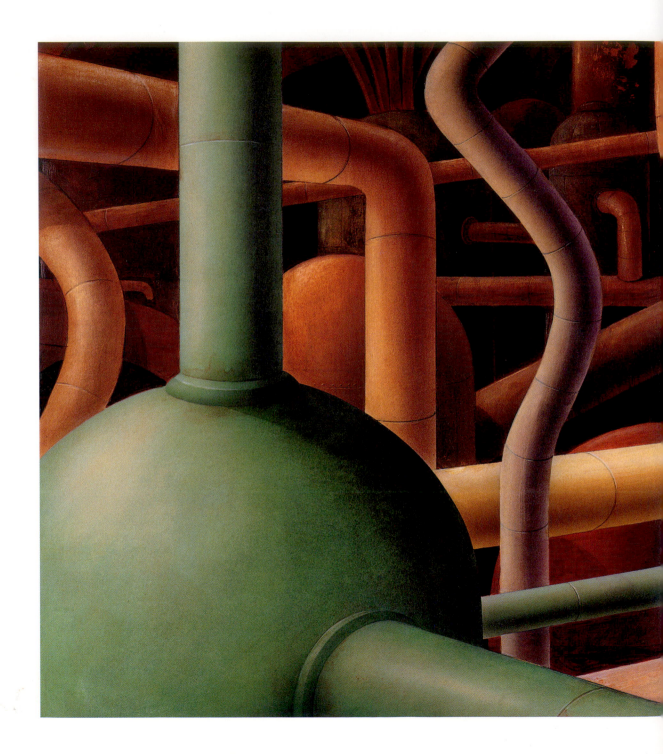

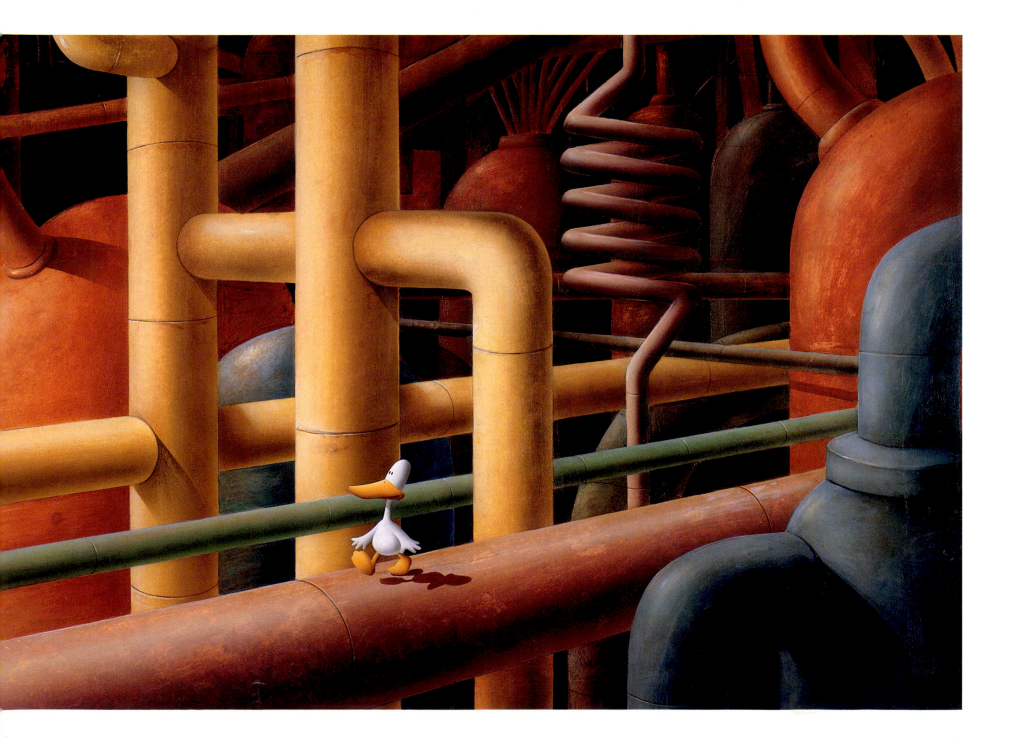

The next thing he knew, the little duck came face to face
with one of the worker alligators, who was very surprised
to see a duck wandering freely about the factory.

Instead of returning the little duck
to the assembly line, the alligator
stuffed him into his lunch box ...

and left the factory.

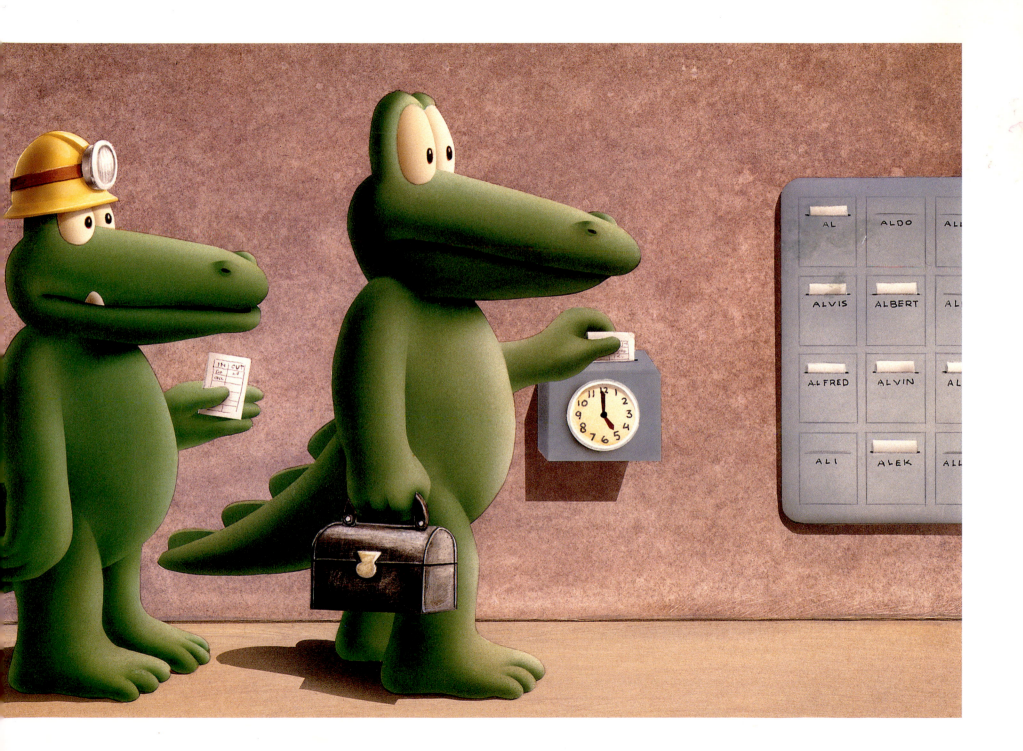

When the little duck emerged from the lunch box, he found himself in a nicely decorated flat. The alligator acted friendly, but all the while he was thinking what a delicious meal the duck would make when properly fattened.

Each day when the
alligator went off to work,
the little duck was left by
himself with a large supply
of tasty snacks. The days
were long and lonely.

At night, the little duck was so delighted to see his big friend that he danced madly about the flat. At first, the alligator was bewildered by this weird welcome, but soon he joined in the crazy dance.

As their friendship grew and grew, the alligator thought less and less about eating the little duck. They even tried going out together, but it proved to be very awkward.

One night, while the alligator worked late at the factory, the little duck contemplated the world outside his window. The alligator had warned him never to venture out alone, but the duck's curiosity got the better of him. He just had to sneak away and explore the streets below.

Further and further
the little duck roamed,
until he was hopelessly
lost and very scared.

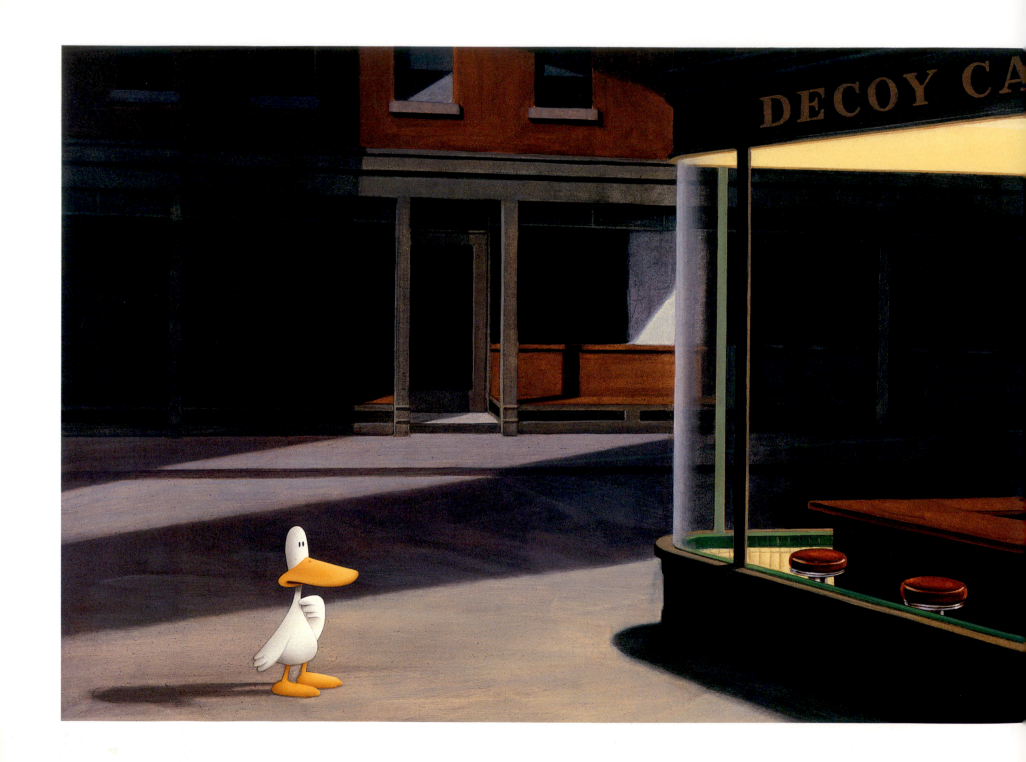

Rounding a corner, the little duck came upon a brightly lit café. His heart leapt when he saw another duck inside. He rushed in and hopped up on to a stool.

"Hey, I'm so glad to see you!" said the little duck breathlessly. "Do you have anything good to eat?"
"Oh, yes," said the waiter duck.

Up popped a huge alligator from behind
the counter.
"WE CERTAINLY DO!"

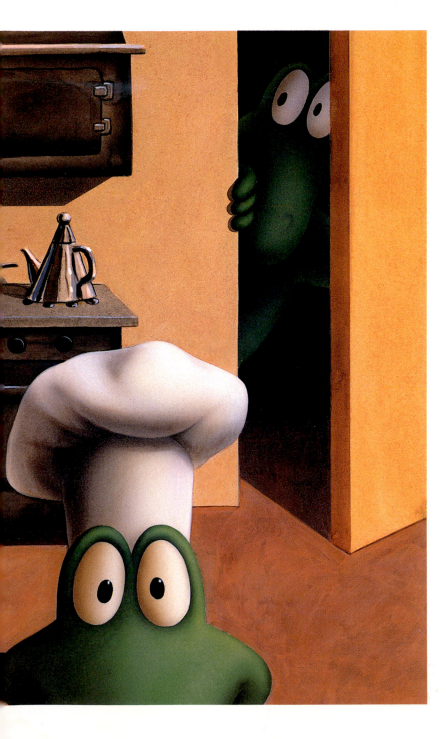

The little duck would have ended up Dish of the Day if his alligator friend had not arrived just in time to rescue him.

Shaken and sleepless after their frightening experience, the duck and the alligator lay awake talking.

"I think I owe you an explanation," said the alligator, and he went on to tell the terrible truth. "After the ducks are hatched at the factory, they are shipped to a part of the city called Ducktown. There they eat and eat until they grow so fat they can't fly away. Eventually, I'm afraid, they end up as the main course in our favourite restaurants."

"Ducks can fly?" asked the little duck. The alligator nodded. The duck was quiet for a while. Then he asked, "Will you take me to Ducktown? I have a plan."

The next day the alligator took the little duck to the edge of Ducktown.
It was very difficult for them to say goodbye.
"Don't worry," said the duck. "It's better this way. Trust me."

The little duck wasted no time spreading the news. At first, nobody would believe his story about the alligators. They thought he was just a troublemaker. But when the little duck showed them the menu from The Decoy Café, the ducks were stunned.

"Listen," the little duck said, "this is what we have to do."

He told the ducks that if they exercised vigorously they would lose weight and become strong. Then they would be able to fly south, where they would be free and safe from the alligators.

Soon the sky was filled with flying ducks. After some practice, they were ready to fly south, just as ducks are supposed to do.

When the alligators looked up and saw their delicious ducks flying away, they were very angry. All except for one alligator, who was very sad.

The alligator was sure he would
never see his little friend again. But
suddenly the duck burst into the
flat with two tickets in his hand.
"I couldn't leave without you."

So, together, they flew south.

The ducks followed the sun to a beautiful, tropical island. They were thrilled to find their little hero waiting for them, but they were very nervous about having an alligator in their midst.

They needn't have worried, though. Mostly, the alligator passed the time dreaming about chicken.

Life was good at the Flapping Arms Seaside Resort.

MICHAEL BEDARD says of *Sitting Ducks*, "The humour in my drawings comes from simple observations of human behaviour and the curious ironies of life."

Born in Canada, Michael has been drawing for as long as he can remember. Although he never attended art school or had any formal training, his distinctive and unique style has catapulted him to widespread fame and he has been an internationally renowned pop artist for over twenty years. He is the creator of hundreds of endearing and wacky characters, the most famous undoubtedly being the Sitting Ducks, initially a poster image which went on to consistently top the list of bestsellers around the world, beating even those of Pablo Picasso! In 1998, the popular ducks progressed from poster to page in this, Bedard's first long-awaited picture book, and are about to star in a full-length animated feature film.

Michael Bedard lives with his family in a small rural community just outside Los Angeles, USA.